This book belongs to

....

First published 2011 by Brown Watson
The Old Mill, 76 Fleckney Road,
Kibworth Beauchamp, Leic LE8 0HG

ISBN: 978-0-7097-1937-3

© 2011 Brown Watson, England
Reprinted 2012 (twice)
Printed in Malaysia

My Ballet Story

Illustrated by Gill Guile

Brown Watson
ENGLAND

Lucy and Megan just love to dance
They skip and run and curtsey and prance,
Off on the way to their first ballet class,
Pirouetting and twirling among flowers and grass.

All the squirrels and rabbits laugh as they say,
"The two little dancers are off on their way!
Shall we skip and hop, and dance along too?"
Birds whistle sweet music; the sky is bright blue.

So Lucy and Megan begin ballet class,
Circling around as they skip and they laugh.
The music is lively . . . and then it is slow;
They dance round the room,
warming up as they go..

8

Next, they all practise their steps at the barre,
Bending their knees, like curtseying stars;
Then pointing their toes, just as they should . . .
Mrs Green says, "Hey! That's really quite good!"

Then they dance to the music the CD is playing
Lucy is skipping; Megan is swaying,
Milo is giggling, "Hey, ballet is fun
And I can jump higher than everyone!"

Then Mrs Green tells them, "I've news for you.
We are doing a concert and you're in it too.
Little dancers like you have a magical glow
And you're the best pupils to put in the show."

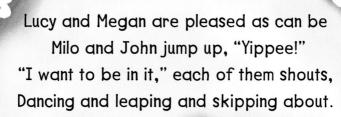

Lucy and Megan are pleased as can be
Milo and John jump up, "Yippee!"
"I want to be in it," each of them shouts,
Dancing and leaping and skipping about.

They all practise hard and are so pleased to find
That all have been chosen with none left behind.
There is much to remember and lots to rehearse.
There are other distractions, but ballet comes first.

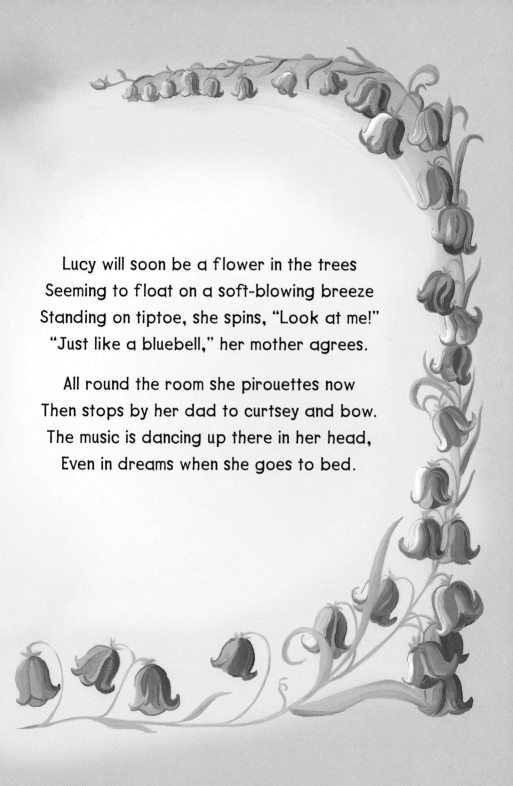

Lucy will soon be a flower in the trees
Seeming to float on a soft-blowing breeze
Standing on tiptoe, she spins, "Look at me!"
"Just like a bluebell," her mother agrees.

All round the room she pirouettes now
Then stops by her dad to curtsey and bow.
The music is dancing up there in her head,
Even in dreams when she goes to bed.

The children work hard
Until the day of the show
So they know what to do when
And just where to go.
They learn how to listen
To the music and beat
And just what to do
With their arms and
their feet.

Now they can feel
the music inside them
As Mrs Green shows
how the rhythm will
guide them.

At last it's the day of the concert and so
They put on their costumes, ready to go.
Milo's an owl who flies out from a tower
Lucy, of course, is a sweet bluebell flower.

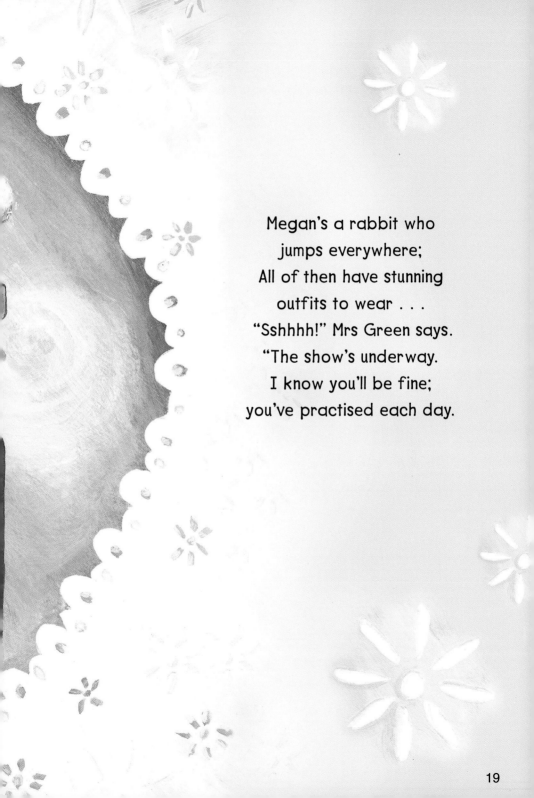

Megan's a rabbit who
jumps everywhere;
All of then have stunning
outfits to wear . . .
"Sshhhh!" Mrs Green says.
"The show's underway.
I know you'll be fine;
you've practised each day.

Come along, Megan, Milo and Lucy too,
Now it's your turn so good luck to you!"
They step onto the stage and into the lights.
When the music starts flowing they grin with delight.

They dance in a woodland;
The moonlight shines bright
As they give their best-ever
Performance tonight.
They almost forget
All those people out there
Until a burst of applause
Fills the night air.

21

Soon all the children
are taking a bow;
With Mrs Green in the wings
clapping too now . . .
As the audience applaud
all the children are sure
They have never been ever
so happy before.

Their parents are cheering;
"Hip Hip Hooray!"
What a wonderful end
to a wonderful day.
Then Mrs Green says,
"What a fabulous show . . .
You're the best little dancers
any teacher could know!"

23

The children all laugh, jumping around,
Excited they haven't let Mrs Green down.
Backstage again, they are grinning with glee
And asking their parents, "Did you watch me?"

Then Megan and Lucy twirl on their toes
And say, "We just LOVE dancing in shows!"

Soon all the children
will skip home to bed
With the magic of ballet
filling their heads.

But first there's a party as they all celebrate
Saying, "Wasn't it BRILL! Wasn't it GREAT!"
They spin and they dance all round the room,
Each dreaming of how they'll be ballet stars soon.

A Few Famous Ballets

Swan Lake

Prince Siegfried falls in love
With a Swan Queen called Odette;
She is the most beautiful creature
The prince has ever met.
Turned into a swan by a sorcerer,
She's spellbound on a magic lake
But the pair are united in
heaven at last
When the evil spell
they break.

The Nutcracker

Little Clara is so excited
When the magic Christmas
Tree grows:
She visits the Land of Sweets
And a wonderful world of snow.
The handsome Nutcracker Prince
And the Sugar Plum Fairy dance
The evil Mouse King is vanquished
As Clara watches it
All, entranced.

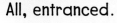

Coppélia

Coppélia the doll
Comes to life upon the stage,
Enchanting all except Swanhilda
Who is in a jealous rage.

The Firebird

Based on a Russian folk tale
From many years ago,
The brilliant firebird dances
In a magic burning glow.